the CRiTTeR club

Marion Takes a Break

by Callie Barkley 💜 illustrated by Marsha Riti

LITTLE SIMON ·
New York London Toronto Sydney New Delhi

Spotlight
ABDO

ABDOPUBLISHING.COM

Reinforced library bound edition published in 2016 by Spotlight, a division of ABDO, PO Box 398166, Minneapolis, Minnesota 55439. Spotlight produces high-quality reinforced library bound editions for schools and libraries. Published by agreement with Little Simon.

Printed in the United States of America, North Mankato, Minnesota.
092015
012016

THIS BOOK CONTAINS RECYCLED MATERIALS

 LITTLE SIMON

An imprint of Simon & Schuster Children's Publishing Division
1230 Avenue of the Americas, New York, New York 10020
Copyright © 2013 by Simon & Schuster, Inc. All rights reserved,
including the right of reproduction in whole or in part in any form.
LITTLE SIMON is a registered trademark of Simon & Schuster, Inc.,
and associated colophon is a trademark of Simon & Schuster, Inc.

LIBRARY OF CONGRESS CATALOGING-IN-PUBLICATION DATA

This book was previously cataloged with the following information:

Barkley, Callie.
Marion takes a break / by Callie Barkley ; illustrated by Marsha Riti. — 1st ed.
  p. cm. — (The Critter Club ; #4)
Summary: When a broken ankle forces Marion to withdraw from the horse show, she finds a way to stay active by helping her friends at the Critter Club animal shelter find homes for a litter of kittens.
ISBN 978-1-4424-6772-9 (pbk) — ISBN 978-1-4424-6773-6 (hc) — ISBN 978-1-4424-6774-3 (eBook)
[1. Fractures—Fiction. 2. Friendship—Fiction. 3. Clubs—Fiction. 4. Animal shelters—Fiction.]
I. Riti, Marsha, ill. II. Title.
PZ7.B250585Mar 2013
[Fic]—dc23
                    2012020390

978-1-61479-433-2 (reinforced library bound edition)

Spotlight
A Division of ABDO
abdopublishing.com

Table of Contents

Chapter 1

Too Much to Do

In the school cafeteria Marion saw Amy, Ellie, and Liz sitting near the window. Marion hurried over. She hoped she would have time to eat her lunch. The recess bell was going to ring in just ten minutes!

"What took you so long?" Amy asked. She scooted down the bench to make space for Marion.

"I couldn't find my lunch!" Marion said, sitting down. "I thought it was in my cubby, but it was actually in my backpack under my ballet shoes and leotard."

I've got to get organized! Marion thought as she started to eat. *Better add that to my to-do list!*

Marion was good at making lists. It helped to keep her busy life in order. Now that it was fall, Marion was busier than ever! She worked very hard in school and always got perfect grades. She also had piano lessons and ballet class every week.

Then there was her horse, Coco. Marion went to the stables at least three times a week. Having a horse was a lot of work, but Marion loved every bit of it.

"So what were you talking about?" Marion asked. She took a big bite of her sandwich.

"The kittens!" Ellie exclaimed. There was a new litter of kittens at The Critter Club, the animal shelter that the four girls helped run in their friend Ms. Sullivan's barn. The girls had met Ms. Sullivan when they found her lost puppy, Rufus.

After that, Ms. Sullivan decided

the town needed an animal shelter. She had an empty barn; Amy's mom, Dr. Purvis, had a lot of advice to offer since she was a veterinarian; and the girls had lots of energy— plus a love of animals.

So The Critter Club began! Since then the girls had helped bunnies and a turtle. They had even done pet sitting over the summer. Now it was up to them to find homes for an entire litter of kittens!

The kittens' mother was a stray cat. When a teacher found them all behind the school, she brought them to the vet clinic. Dr. Purvis had suggested that the five healthy kittens stay at The

Critter Club, and the girls were very excited to help take care of them!

"The mother cat and one kitten are still at the clinic," Amy told her friends. "My mom said that the mama cat needs more rest. And even though the tabby kitten's injured paw is getting better, he still needs to heal for a while longer too."

The girls took turns helping out at The Critter Club after school and on weekends. "Liz and I had such a great time at the club yesterday afternoon. Those kittens are just so cute!" Ellie squealed.

"That's the thing," Amy said, "it should be easy to find homes for them. I was thinking . . . what if we have a big party at The Critter Club? People could come meet the kittens!"

Marion, Ellie, and Liz all nodded. "That's a great idea!" said

Liz. "Everyone would see how cute they are!"

"We could have music!" Ellie suggested. She loved to perform. "I could sing!"

"We could get dressed up!" Marion added. She had a silver dress that would be perfect.

"We could put up pretty lights—and some artwork!" said Liz. She was an amazing artist.

Marion imagined how wonderful Liz's paintings would look hanging around The Critter Club. They would really jazz up the barn!

Just then the recess bell rang. Marion chewed fast, trying to finish her sandwich. Then the four friends headed outside. It was autumn in Santa Vista, but in their part of California, it never got too cold.

Amy walked next to Marion. "Maybe we'll think of more party ideas this afternoon," said Amy.

"This afternoon?" Marion mumbled. Her mouth was still full.

"Yeah, at The Critter Club?" Amy said. "It's Monday—our day to help out. Remember?"

Marion had forgotten! It wasn't like her to get her schedule mixed up. "Uh? The Critter Club? Of course I will be there!"

Marion Makes a Mess

If we finish early, I'll have time to ride Coco before dinner, Marion was thinking.

"Marion, I think you fed that kitten already," Amy was saying.

Marion looked down. The light gray kitten wasn't drinking. He didn't seem interested in Marion's bottle of milk. "Oh! You're right!"

Marion exclaimed. "What am I doing?"

She and Amy were at The Critter Club, feeding the tiny kittens.

Dr. Purvis had told them that the kittens were only about five weeks old! Feeding such young cats was tricky. Luckily, Dr. Purvis had shown the girls just what to do. She

had even made them a poster to
remind them of the steps.

♡ How to Feed the Kittens ♡

Step 1: Take out one container marked "Kitten Milk" from the refrigerator. This is special milk that is just like their mother's.

Step 2: Pour the milk into a clean baby bottle.

Step 3: Warm the bottle in the bottle warmer until light turns green.

Step 4: Hold kitten, sitting up, in your lap, or let kitten lie on his/her belly while eating. Do not cradle kitten belly up like a baby.

Marion and Amy had come to the club right after school. Marion had been rushing around ever since. She really wanted to get to the stables to ride Coco. They had a big competition coming up. Marion and Coco had won it last year, and

Marion had her sights on taking the blue ribbon again this year. There was a good reason blue was her favorite color!

The only thing was, they would need some extra practice if they wanted to win.

Marion warmed a bottle for the black kitten. But hurrying across the barn, she dropped it on the barn floor and had to make up a new one. Then she knocked over the bottle warmer, spilling the water inside. Next, Marion didn't screw a bottle top on tight enough. Some milk spilled on the white kitten.

"Oh, for goodness' sake!" she cried. "I just can't do anything right!"

Amy came over. "Marion, are you okay?" Amy asked kindly. "You don't seem like yourself."

She's right, thought Marion. *I'm not myself. I never, ever mess up this*

much! Marion was used to getting things right the first time.

She sighed and wiped up the milk. "I'm fine," she said. "Just in a rush!" She looked up at Amy. "I need to get to the stables before dinner. We have a competition coming up,

and Coco and I need some extra practice."

Amy smiled. "Oh, I get it now," she said. "Well, I can finish up here if you need to go."

Marion studied Amy's face. "Really?" Marion asked. "Are you sure?"

Amy looked around. "We're almost done anyway," she said. "Really! You should go. Say hi to Coco for me!"

Marion felt so lucky to have such a great best friend. She gave Amy a huge hug. "Thank you!" she said as she turned to go. "You are the best!"

Chapter 3

One Wrong Step

That afternoon Marion rode Coco until the sun started to set.

The next day, Tuesday, she headed to the stables right after school. She and Coco worked on walk, trot, canter, and gallop all afternoon.

Then on Wednesday afternoon Marion had her riding lesson. She and her teacher worked on some low jumps.

By Thursday Marion was starting to feel ready. "We've got two more weeks, Coco," she said to her pretty brown horse. Marion was brushing Coco in her stall. "Two weeks until the show. I know we can do it."

She looked over at the stall door. Coco's

ribbons hung in a row. "We'll get you another blue ribbon to hang up!"

Marion said good-bye to Coco before heading to the changing room. She *loved* her riding outfit—her tall boots, her breeches, her crisp, navy blue jacket, but Marion also loved what she'd worn to school that day. It was her *favorite fall outfit*: her corduroy skirt, lavender cardigan, purple tights, and purple flats. She was excited to put them back on!

"Marion!" a voice called from outside her dressing cubby. "Are you there?" Marion knew that voice. It was her six-year-old sister, Gabby. She took riding lessons at the stable too. Gabby was going to compete in the junior division at the horse show. "Come on! Mom and I are waiting in the car!"

"Uh, I'm coming!" Marion called. She hurried to pull on

her tights, but pulling on tights fast was very hard to do. Marion stepped into her flats and hurried outside. She saw her mom's car by the corral fence. Marion ran across the stable yard.

Halfway there she stepped in a dip in the gravel path. Her left foot twisted in a strange way when she landed.

"Ow!" Marion cried. She felt a sharp pain in her ankle. Her leg gave out and she fell onto the gravel. "Ow! My ankle!" It felt so weird—and hurt *so much*!

When Marion didn't get up, Marion's mom and sister ran over from the car.

What happened next was a big blur. Marion's mom and sister helped her up, but she couldn't walk. Standing on her ankle hurt

way too much so Marion's mom gave her a piggyback ride to the car. They drove straight to the hospital, where Marion's dad, a doctor, met them in the emergency room.

Dr. Ballard examined her ankle and ordered an X-ray. Marion began to worry.

Before long, Marion's dad put

his hand on her shoulder. He held the X-ray up to the light.

"Bad news, kiddo. It looks like you have a pretty bad sprain," he said. "You're going to need a cast."

"A *cast*?" Marion was shocked. "For how long?"

"At least three weeks—maybe four," her dad said. "You'll have crutches to help you get around, but you will need to take it easy for a while. But guess what? Casts come in all kinds of cool colors!"

For once Marion didn't care about fashion. She couldn't believe

what she was hearing. This *wasn't* happening! "No, no, no! I can't be in a cast for three weeks! Dad, the horse show is in *two weeks*!"

Her dad put down the X-ray. He

took Marion's hand. "I'm really sorry, honey," he said. "It's going to take time for your ankle to heal." He sighed a big sigh. "I'm afraid the horse show is out."

Chapter 4

Friends to the Rescue!

Marion closed her book and tossed it onto the sofa. She just *couldn't* concentrate.

It was Friday afternoon. She'd had the cast less than twenty-four hours, and already she was tired of it. She had missed school because she wasn't used to walking with the crutches yet.

"By Monday you'll be a pro," her dad had said that morning. "Then you can try them at school."

Monday couldn't come soon enough for Marion. *I'm missing everything!* she thought. *I can't go to ballet next week. I can't ride Coco. I don't even know what's going on in math class!*

Marion's mom was home with her, so Marion's dad picked up Gabby from her riding lesson at the stables. She walked in with her riding clothes still on. Marion

couldn't help feeling envious.

What's worse than not being able to ride in the horse show? she asked herself. *Having a sister who is riding in the horse show.* Marion knew it wasn't her sister's fault. Still, it was going to be *so* hard to watch Gabby ride when Marion couldn't.

Just then the doorbell rang. Marion heard her mom open the front door. Moments later Amy, Ellie, and Liz poked their heads in to the family room. "Can we come in?" Amy asked.

"*Yes!*" Marion cried. She was so glad to see her friends.

Ellie handed Marion a very pretty bouquet of flowers. "At school Mrs. Sienna told the class about your ankle!" Ellie said.

"We had to come see you," added Liz. She gave Marion a get-well card she had made.

"We thought you might need cheering up," said Amy. "Oh, and these." She handed Marion a tin. Marion opened the lid. Inside were Amy's mother's famous oatmeal raisin cookies. They were Marion's favorite.

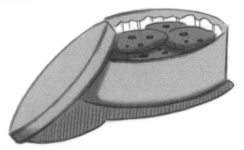

Marion forced a smile. "Thanks, guys," she said. She put the flowers, the card, and the cookies next to her on the coffee table.

"Wait," said Amy. "Aren't you going to have a cookie?"

Marion shrugged. "Not right now," she said with a big sigh. "I'm not hungry."

Amy looked at Ellie and Liz. "Uh-oh," Amy said. "Not hungry for her favorite cookies? She *does* need to be cheered up."

Ellie giggled. "Well, then, let's tell her," she said. "Listen, Marion. About the sleepover tonight—"

Marion slapped her forehead as it hit her. "The sleepover!" she cried. "Today is Friday! I forgot!"

The four girls had a sleepover almost every Friday night. They each took turns hosting. Marion knew that this week it was at Liz's house.

"Oh," she groaned, *"another thing I can't do!"* She wasn't feeling up to getting off the sofa—not until she could practice more with her crutches.

"Yeah," said Amy. "We thought you might not be able to come to Liz's."

"So we brought the sleepover to you!" said Liz.

Marion gasped. "Really?" she said. "You mean we can have it here instead?"

"Sure!" Liz said. "I'll host next week instead. Now, you've got to let me sign your cast!"

"Ooh! Me too!" said Amy.

"Me three!" said Ellie.

"Sure!" Marion said. Then she smiled—for real this time.

Chapter 5

Back to School?

On Monday morning Marion woke up feeling excited. After practicing with her crutches all weekend, her mom and dad had agreed she could go back to school!

Marion hopped on her good foot to her closet. She wanted to pick out the perfect outfit.

Then she realized something.

She couldn't wear tights or leggings. They wouldn't fit over her cast. And—Marion gasped—she could only wear one shoe!

None of my favorite outfits will look as good with this cast! she thought.

Marion had to wear her least favorite jeans. And for her one shoe, her mom wanted her to wear a sneaker. "Comfort and grip. That's what you need!" Mrs. Ballard said.

Marion checked her outfit in the mirror. "This day is not off to a good start," she said grumpily.

At school things didn't get much better. It took her forever to get from the drop-off circle to her classroom. She was the last one in her seat. Marion hated being last.

In gym class Marion couldn't play kickball. She had to sit on the bench and watch. Amy, Liz, and Ellie took turns keeping her company.

At lunchtime Marion couldn't carry her lunchbox *and* walk on crutches at the same time. Amy was happy to carry her lunch for her, but Marion didn't like the feeling of not being able to do things on her own.

As the week went on, Marion got more frustrated. At her piano lesson her cast made it hard to use the foot pedal. None of Marion's songs sounded right.

At ballet class, all the students were learning new moves. Marion went so she could at least see the steps. But

she couldn't practice them. *Wow, everyone looks so graceful,* she thought. She wished she were up there, right in front.

Hardest of all was visiting Coco. The stables were very busy with riders getting ready for the horse show.

Marion fed Coco a carrot and brushed her mane. "I'm so sorry, Coco," she whispered. "You have worked so hard to win. I'm just a huge failure—at everything."

Chapter 6

Broken Dreams

Finally it was Thursday—Marion's and Amy's turn after school at The Critter Club. *At last!* thought Marion. *Feeding the little kittens is something fun that even I can do with this cast!*

It turned out this wasn't exactly true. Marion couldn't get around on crutches while holding a kitten in her arms. And she definitely couldn't get around with a kitten *and* a bottle.

"That's okay," said Amy. "We'll feed them together. You hold this one. I'll get the bottle."

That's when Marion's frustration bubbled over. "I can't do anything

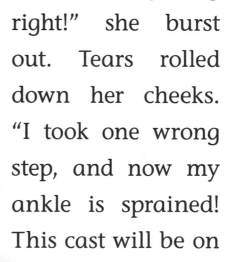

right!" she burst out. Tears rolled down her cheeks. "I took one wrong step, and now my ankle is sprained! This cast will be on for weeks. And everything keeps on going without me! I'll never be able to catch up!"

She covered her face with her hands and sobbed. Amy hugged her tight.

"Oh, Marion, it's okay! You're going to be better so soon!" Amy said. "You make it sound like

everything is a big race, but it isn't. You don't have to be number one all the time."

Amy let go of Marion. She looked her right in the eye. "You know, we all love you for *you*," Amy said. "It's not because you get awesome grades, or

play piano amazingly . . . or dance like a pro . . . or win blue ribbons with Coco. Should I keep going?"

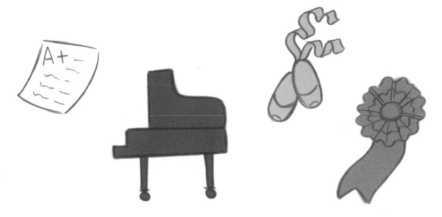

Marion laughed through her tears. "No, that's okay," she said.

Amy smiled. "It must be really hard not to be able to do your favorite things, but maybe, for now, just think of the things you *can* do."

Amy looked down at the kittens. "Like feed these fuzz balls."

Marion wiped her tears. She took a deep breath. "You're right," she said with a smile. "Thanks, Amy."

Then, the girls fed the kittens—together.

Chapter 7

The Plan

The next day at school Amy had great news.

"Mom says the kitten with the injured paw is doing much better!" she told the girls at lunch. "He can go home—well, he could if he had a home."

"Yeah," said Liz. "Too bad none of the kittens have been adopted.

Hey! He could come stay at The Critter Club too, right?"

"Great idea, Liz!" Ellie said.

Amy nodded. "He might need some special care for a little while, but we can handle that. Right?"

"Right!" the others chimed in.

"And while he gets stronger," said Marion, "we can work on finding homes for *all* the kittens!"

Marion was feeling more like

her old self again. Her talk with Amy had helped a lot. She got out a notebook and pen to start a to-do list.

"So what about Amy's idea?" Marion asked. "Having a big party at The Critter Club so people can meet the kittens?"

"I still love that idea," said Ellie.

"There's just one thing," said Liz. "Throwing a big party costs money. We'd have to buy food and decorations."

"That's true," Amy agreed. "It could get pretty expensive."

Marion thought it over. How could they get lots of people to meet the kittens? She remembered when they were trying to find homes for

some bunnies. Ellie was starring in the school play. She had gotten the bunnies up on stage.

Could we get the kittens in some kind of show? thought Marion. *A show . . . A show . . .* Then it hit her. *The horse show!*

"I've got it!" Marion exclaimed. "We could bring the kittens to the big horse show next weekend! We

could set up a booth. There will be lots of kids and parents there!"

"Yes!" said Amy. "Marion, that's a *great* idea. Maybe my mom could bake some cookies for us to give away to people so they stop by the booth!"

"I could bring my karaoke machine!" Ellie chimed in.

"Ellie," began Liz, "you are a *fantastic* singer, but—"

"Oh no!" Ellie said. "Not so I can sing. We

could use the microphone to get people's attention."

Liz giggled. "Oh! That makes sense. And I can be in charge of decorating the booth."

Suddenly Marion knew what *she* wanted to be in charge of. "Can I make a special collar for each kitten?" she asked. "That way they'll each look their best for the big day."

The girls agreed it was a plan—a *great* plan!

Chapter 8

The Sixth Kitten

Marion lined up the kittens' collars she had made so far. "Five down, one to go!" she said.

She was at The Critter Club with Amy, Ellie, and Liz. All four had been spending extra time there. The horse show was only three days away, and there was a lot they wanted to get organized.

"Wow, Marion! Those are all so pretty!" Ellie said.

"Thanks!" Marion replied. She had worked hard on her creations. She had thought a lot about which color would look best on each kitten. "The braided

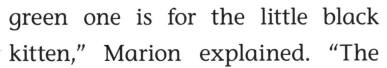

green one is for the little black kitten," Marion explained. "The

bright purple satin collar is for the white kitten. The red velvet will look great

on the black and white kitten, and the pink collar will really stand out on the silver kitten. The sunny yellow collar goes on the dark gray kitten." *Whew!* Marion took a breath.

"Great colors!" said Liz. "What about the tabby kitten?"

The tabby kitten was the one with the healing paw. Marion was saving his collar for last. "I've got something extraspecial planned for Ollie," Marion said with a smile.

The name had been Marion's suggestion. All the girls gave Ollie extra care and cuddles, but Marion had a special place in her heart for him. His brothers and sisters could now run and jump and play. But poor Ollie was still limping around a little. He would often sit off to the side and watch the others.

Sometimes Marion felt like she and Ollie were going through the same thing.

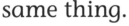

Marion reached for her clipboard. She checked the list. "So what's left to do before Saturday?" she asked.

"Mom and I are baking another batch of cookies tonight," said Amy. "We've got six dozen so far! We're going to bring a big cooler of lemonade, too."

"Great!" said Marion, making a note on her list. "Food, check!"

"And I've got almost all of the

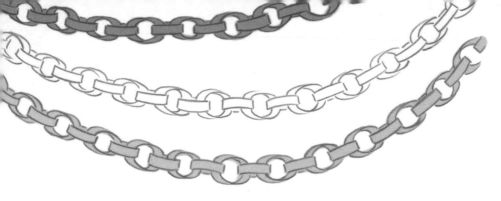

decorations ready," said Liz. "I'm still making some really long paper chains in bright colors. We can hang them all around the sides of our table. Tonight I'll make the sign!"

"And Mom helped me put new batteries in my karaoke

machine," Ellie added. "Now I'm thinking up catchy things to say at the horse show. What do you think of this?" Ellie held an imaginary microphone to her mouth. *"Kittens and cookies! Cookies and kittens!"* she boomed.

The girls laughed at Ellie's announcer voice. "That will get people's attention, all right!" Amy said.

Marion checked things off on the list. "Decorations, check! Karaoke machine, check!"

There was one other thing Marion wondered about. "Guys, how will we know who *should* adopt a kitten—who would give them a good home?" Marion wanted to make sure the kittens would be taken care of.

"Good thinking, Marion," Amy said. "My mom will be there the whole time, so she can talk to people about having kittens as pets."

Marion nodded. She knew that

Dr. Purvis would make sure the kittens went to loving families.

She hated the idea of any of the kittens living somewhere they wouldn't be loved . . . especially little Ollie.

Chapter 9

Kittens and Cookies

"Wow!" said Liz, leaning close to Marion. "There are a lot of people here!" She had to speak up. Right next to them Ellie was half talking, half singing into the karaoke machine microphone. She couldn't quite contain her musical side.

"Kittens and cookies! Come have a looksie!"

"Lots of people *and* lots of horses!" Marion replied to Liz.

The horse show was being held at the Santa Vista fairgrounds— near Ms. Sullivan's house. There were two big performance rings, and stands for people to sit and watch. The parking lot was full of cars and horse trailers.

The girls and their parents had come early. They had picked a shady spot, between the parking lot and the performance area, where they had set up the booth. It was made out of Marion's family's beach

umbrella and Liz's family's big folding table. With Liz's decorations and sign, the girls thought it looked great!

The kittens were playing happily in a little fenced area behind the table. Ms. Sullivan had brought them over from The Critter Club.

Earlier Marion had put on their special new collars.

"They all look sooo cute!" Ellie squealed. "And I love Ollie's collar, Marion."

Marion liked it too. It was a sparkly silver ribbon with a heart charm on the front. The other girls couldn't see, but on the back of the charm was a message.

To OLLIE, LOVE ALWAYS, MARION.

It had already been a busy morning! Lots of people were stopping by the booth. Some just stopped by for cookies and lemonade, but many others asked Dr. Purvis about adopting a kitten. Amy's mom was chatting nonstop!

Right before noon Marion took a

break. It was almost Gabby's turn in the ring! She went with her mom and dad to watch from the stands. It *was* hard to watch her sister ride, but not because she was jealous. She was nervous and *excited* for her little sister!

As Gabby did her routine, Marion was amazed—her sister was great! When Gabby finished, Marion cheered louder than anyone.

Back at The Critter Club booth,

Marion could hardly wait to tell her friends.

"She and her horse both looked so calm. Their walk, trot, canter, and gallop was the best I've seen them do!" Then Marion noticed that there were only three kittens in the little play area. "What happened to the black, the white, and the silver kittens?"

Dr. Purvis smiled. "Three of the families from this morning came back," she said. "They wanted to adopt. I'm sure they will give our little friends great homes!"

Marion smiled happily. Secretly, though, she was glad none of the families had chosen Ollie. She would have been sad to have missed saying good-bye.

The hours sped by. More people stopped by the booth. One by one the cookies disappeared and the lemonade cooler got emptier. Ellie's voice had gotten tired, too, and she had turned off the karaoke machine.

The Critter Club Presents, Meet the Kittens!

Before Marion knew it, two more kittens had been adopted—Ollie was the only one left.

The horse show was almost done. The loudspeaker came on, and Marion could hear a voice reading a list of winners. *Last year they read my name,* she thought sadly. *Not this year.*

Just then Marion *did* hear her

name announced!

"The junior division blue ribbon goes to rider number fourteen, Ballard." That was Marion's last name! Then the announcer went on: "Congratulations to Gabby Ballard!"

Marion gasped and clapped. Her sister had won a blue ribbon!

Chapter 10

Surprise!

What a day! The girls had found homes for five kittens *and* Gabby had won!

"I'm so proud of you!" Marion said to her little sister. She gave Gabby a great big hug. At that moment seeing her sister win was even better than getting her own blue ribbon!

"Let's celebrate!" said Marion's mom. She invited all the girls, their parents, and Ms. Sullivan back to their house for dinner.

Together everyone packed up the booth. It took Marion's dad a few extra minutes to get the umbrella back in their car. Then Marion and Gabby and their parents were on their way home—with Ollie. He sat, all alone, in a cat carrier at Marion's feet.

"Don't worry, Ollie, we'll find you a home," she said to him.

The Ballards were the last to

arrive at their own house. Marion's dad and sister took Ollie inside. Marion's mom got the crutches from the trunk. She helped Marion out of the car and up the walk.

When Marion hopped through the front door, she couldn't believe her eyes. There were balloons everywhere! There was a big cake on the coffee table. A colorful banner hung over the fireplace.

"Surprise!" everyone shouted. There was Amy, Liz, Ellie, and their parents; Liz's big brother, Stewart; Ellie's little brother, Toby; Ellie's nana Gloria; Ms. Sullivan; and Rufus, too! They were all looking at Marion!

"A party . . . for *me*?" Marion asked in shock. "But Gabby is the one who won."

Marion's mom gave Gabby a squeeze. "Yes, but now it's a party for you *and* Gabby!" she said. "We're very proud of you *both*, Marion."

Marion's dad put an arm around

her shoulders. "We know nothing has been easy with the cast," he said. "Missing the horse show was really tough, but you made the best of it. You put your efforts into working hard for The Critter Club."

He looked around at the girls. "All of you did . . . and it really paid off."

Marion felt great. Actually, she felt better than great. She felt *proud*. She hadn't won anything or gotten a perfect grade. Instead, she knew she had done an important job. "Finding homes for five kittens in one day *is* pretty awesome!" she said happily.

"You can make that six," said Marion's mom. She was holding Ollie.

Marion's smile disappeared from her face. "Six?" she said. "Has . . . has Ollie been adopted too?" Marion prepared for the bad news.

"Yep!" her mom said. "He's been adopted by . . ."

"*Us!*" said Marion's dad and sister together.

Marion's eyes went wide. One of her crutches fell over. She almost lost her balance but didn't. "Do you mean it?" she cried. "Really? Really, *really*?"

Marion's mom and dad smiled. "We really mean it," her dad said. "But there's one other person who has to agree."

Marion looked around in surprise. "Who?" she asked.

Her parents glanced over at Dr. Purvis.

"I can't think of a better home for little Ollie," Dr. Purvis said with a smile.

As Marion sat down on the couch, her mother handed Ollie to her. The rest of the girls gathered

around Marion and hugged her
and the adorable kitten.

"As soon as my ankle is all
better, we're going to have lots of
adventures together, Ollie!" Marion
told the kitten.

Ollie purred and nestled
happily into Marion's lap.

COLLECT THEM ALL!

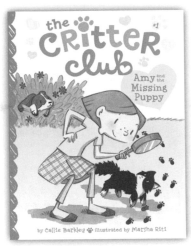

**Hardcover Book ISBN
978-1-61479-430-1**

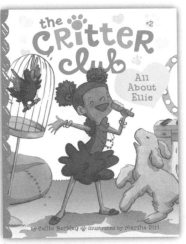

**Hardcover Book ISBN
978-1-61479-431-8**

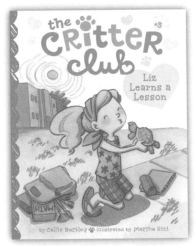

**Hardcover Book ISBN
978-1-61479-432-5**

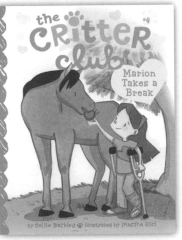

**Hardcover Book ISBN
978-1-61479-433-2**

BARKL   **FLT**
Barkley, Callie.
Marion takes a break /

03/16